W9-AAA-856

SEE MOM RUN

Kara Douglass Thom

Illustrated by Lilly Golden

BREAKAWAY BOOKS
HALCOTTSVILLE, NEW YORK
2003

For all mothers who move—who have inspired their children, and me.
—KDT

For Isabel and Rose, who run wild.
—LG

SEE MOM RUN
Copyright © 2003 by Kara Douglass Thom
Illustrations copyright © 2003 by Lilly Golden

ISBN: 1-891369-40-7

Printed in China

Published by Breakaway Books
P.O. Box 24
Halcottsville, NY 12438
(800) 548-4348
www.breakawaybooks.com

FIRST PRINTING

The first thing Penny saw when she opened her eyes was the medal hanging on her bedpost.

She put the medal around her neck after she got dressed.

Penny ate breakfast.

Penny brushed her teeth.

Penny rode the bus to school.

"My mommy ran a marathon yesterday," she said in front of her class. "When she finished she got this medal."

"What's a marathon?" asked her classmate Jacob.

"A marathon is a race where lots of people run far," said Penny.

"How far?" asked her friend Rachel. "A whole mile?"

"No! Much farther!" Penny told her. "A marathon is more than 26 miles."

"That's farther than my grandmother's house," said Andrew.

"Yeah, mine, too," said Mary.

"Did your mommy win?" asked Nathan.

"No, she was almost *last*," said Penny. "Lots of people finished in front of her, and we waited a long time at the finish line."

Penny remembered how big her mommy's smile was as she finished the race.

"Then why did she get a medal?" asked Thomas.

"Because everyone who tries hard and crosses the finish line is a winner. That's what my mommy says. She says I helped her. That's why she gave me her medal."

"Oh, yeah?" said Tyler.
"Did you run the race
with her?"

"Well, no. But I trained with her."

"I timed her laps at the track."

"I helped her work out at the gym."

"I taught her a lot about stretching."

"I put her shoes out on the porch to dry."

"I raced her at the beach."

"I gave her back rubs sometimes."

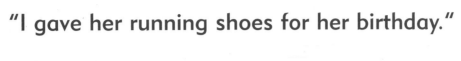

"I gave her running shoes for her birthday."

"I helped her cool down after runs on hot days."

"I cheered for her when she raced."

"She said we made a good team."

"Some day, I'm going to run like her."